Dedicated to Rowena, Theadora, and Robyn. Without the support of family, greatness can never be achieved.

Contents

Chapter 1: The City's Shadow — Page 4.

Chapter 2: Echoes of the Past — Page 9.

Chapter 3: A Nobleman's Burden — Page 13.

Chapter 4: Birth of the Watcher — Page 17.

Chapter 5: The First Dawn — Page 21.

Chapter 6: A Legacy of Justice — Page 25.

Chapter 7: Shadows of Whitechapel — Page 30.

Chapter 8: The Lady — Page 34.

Chapter 9: Conflicted Alliances — Page 43.

Chapter 10: The Hidden Sanctuary — Page 49.

Chapter 11: A Darker Turn — Page 53.

Chapter 12: Collision Course — Page 58.

Chapter 13: The Watcher and The Ripper — Page 63.

Chapter 14: The Night's End — Page 69.

Chapter 15: Dawn of The Watcher — Page 77.

Epilogue: Echoes of Tomorrow — Page 81.

THE WATCHER OF WESTMINSTER

ECHOES OF THE NIGHT

Chapter 1:
The City's Shadow

In the mist-laden alleys of London, in 1888, the city lay draped in a shroud of contrasts. The affluent West End, bathed in the warm glow of gas lamps, stood in stark contrast to the desolate East End, where shadows clung to every corner like cobwebs.

Outside the Palace of Westminster, Edward Langley, a man in his early thirties, stood surveying the cityscape. His pale blue eyes, sharp and discerning, roved over the sprawling city — a city that never truly slept, echoing with the whispers of both its glorious and sinister tales, which could almost be heard as you travel through its labyrinth of narrow streets and dimly lit pubs.

The East End had been Edward's childhood home. It was there, amidst the raucous clamour of the marketplace and the dingy corners of alleyways, that his life had changed forever. Twenty years earlier, a young Edward, a boy of only 10 years of age, played in the dirty streets of the East End with his best friends, Thomas Finley and Matthew Reed. The three were inseparable, never seen apart, sharing dreams of a future far removed from the poverty that surrounded them. Matthew would often tell them "One day Eddie, I'm going to live there and you and Tommy can come too" as he pointed over the murky Thames at the palace of Westminster that sat in the shadow of Big Ben.

"You'll live in the Tower of London more like" Thomas and Edward would joke back. Their life was simple, and they wanted for much, but they were happy.

However, one fateful evening, Edward's innocent world was shattered. He was walking to meet Thomas and Matthew at their usual spot, a small alley just behind a bakery, the old woman who owned it, Agnes would often give them small cakes or treats and laugh at them playing. But as Edward approached the alley, he did not hear Agnes' laughter but instead a blood-curdling scream, Edward ran forward, his dark hair sweeping in front of his eyes, and as he reached the meeting point it became clear. Thomas was at the meeting point, but he was not playing. He lay on his back on the mud-covered cobbles, his young life snuffed out with brutal swiftness. A single deep slash across his throat. His skin was a pallid grey and his blood ran through the cracks in the cobbles like red rivers.

Edward thought about that day often, the crime remained unsolved to this day. Edward didn't see Matthew much after that either, their respective parents keeping them off the streets. It wasn't long before the east end continued to bustle and drone on like nothing had ever happened. This event had left Edward with a gaping wound in his heart and an unyielding thirst for justice — a burning desire for truth, a flame that had only grown stronger with time.

The tragedy propelled Edward into a different life. His father now determined to get his son out of the east end worked harder than ever. Over the following years, he had managed to rent a warehouse and was quickly dealing with a large number of imports into the east end of London, he became a man of considerable influence and wealth, and at his first opportunity, he took Edward away from the East End, aiming to shield him from further harm.

As Edward grew, he was groomed for a life of nobility. His father continued to build his empire eventually being made a Lord. He was a stern but fair man, he instilled in Edward a strong sense of moral duty.

"Our privilege comes with a responsibility," his father often said, a mantra that Edward took to heart. Little did his father know how deeply these words would influence Edward. He thought of this often since his father's recent passing.

Now, as a renowned nobleman himself, Edward's days were filled with the trappings of wealth and privilege. Yet, as night fell, his true passion came to life. Hidden away in his study, walls lined with newspaper clippings and maps of the city, Edward pored over the unsolved crimes that plagued London. The recent string of brutal murders in Whitechapel had captured his attention most of all, the nature of the killings was so reminiscent of poor Thomas. The police seemed powerless; the crimes unsolvable. But Edward now felt a stirring within him, the murders had triggered a call to action that he could no longer ignore. As the chimes of Big Ben echoed through the night, marking the late hour, a determination settled over Edward. The city needed more than what the law could offer. It needed a guardian, a Watcher, one who could navigate both the light and the shadows, Edward had been planning for months desperately finding the courage and drive to do what he felt needed to be done, he had spent many a long night toiling over ideas and designs, but now Turning from the vista of the city, Edward Langley stepped back into the shadows of the Palace, his mind racing with plans. The time for action was fast approaching, but was he ready to take the necessary steps to save his city.

Chapter 2:

Echoes of the Past

In the heart of London's aristocratic West End, amidst grand estates and manicured gardens, stood Langley Manor. It was a stark contrast to the East End, where Edward had spent his formative years.

Now, in his spacious study at his Manor, surrounded by volumes of law and history, Edward's thoughts often drifted back to Thomas and the East End. It was a stark reminder of the city's failure to protect its most vulnerable. This memory was what drove him to pore over every detail of the recent Whitechapel murders, seeking patterns and clues overlooked by the police.

Edward's obsession did not go unnoticed. His butler, Mr. Humphrey, a loyal servant to the Langley family for years, observed Edward's nightly vigils with a growing concern. He remembered the young, carefree boy Edward once was and worried about the path he was now treading. Yet, up until now, out of respect and a deep sense of loyalty, he had remained silent, offering support in his discreet way.

One evening, as Edward sat immersed in his research, Mr. Humphrey entered with a tray of tea. "You should rest, sir," he suggested gently, placing the tray on the desk.

Edward looked up, his eyes tired but resolute. "Rest cannot be afforded, not while the city suffers under such injustice," he replied, his voice tinged with a passion that went beyond mere concern.

Mr. Humphrey nodded, understanding his master's drive, yet worried about its consequences.

"If I may be so bold sir," Mr Humphrey said cautiously "you spend every night locked away in this study, staring into the very darkest corners of London. What is it you intend to achieve?"

Edward hesitated "The police are at a loss Humphrey, maybe I can find something they have missed, maybe I can help solve these atrocities" he responded with determination in his voice.

"With all due respect sir," Mr Humphrey said sternly "how do you expect to make a difference from the comfort of your study?" a look of anger flashed across Edward's face.

"You forget yourself Mr Humphery" Edward Snapped.

"I do apologize, I have overstepped" Mr Humphrey replied sheepishly "Just remember, sir, to not lose yourself in this pursuit," he advised before leaving the room.

Alone again, Edward's gaze fell upon a newspaper headline about the latest Whitechapel victim. A sense of urgency washed over him. Mr Humphrey was right; Edward knew that he couldn't make a real difference from his stately home and he couldn't stand idly by while his city bled. It was time for a new approach, it was time for The Watcher.

As the clock struck midnight, Edward Langley made a decision that would forever change the course of his life and the streets of London.

Chapter 3:

The Nobleman's Burden

In the seclusion of Langley Manor, behind the facade of opulence and tradition, Edward Langley grappled with a secret that strained the very fibres of his noble existence. By day, he was the epitome of a Victorian gentleman, attending social events and managing family affairs. But as night fell, his true self emerged, driven by a purpose that transcended his aristocratic duties.

One evening, as Edward sat in his study, his eyes once again wandered over the maps of London and the clippings of unsolved crimes that adorned his walls. The glaring disparity between his life of privilege and the plight of those in the East End weighed heavily on his conscience. His thoughts were interrupted by the soft knock of Mr. Humphrey.

"Sir, your presence is requested at the Marquess of Collingwood's ball next week," Mr. Humphrey announced, handing Edward the invitation.

Edward glanced at the invitation, his mind elsewhere. "Thank you, Humphrey. Please send our acceptance," he replied absently.

Mr. Humphrey, sensing his master's preoccupation, hesitated. "Sir, if I may be so bold, you've been rather... preoccupied of late. Is there anything amiss?"

Edward looked up, a faint smile touching his lips. "Just the usual concerns of our city, Humphrey. Nothing for you to worry about."

Yet worry was precisely what Mr. Humphrey felt. He had seen the transformation in Edward – the late nights, the intense focus on criminal activities, the growing detachment from his societal role. But he respected Edward's privacy, offering a nod of understanding before leaving the room.

Alone again, Edward's gaze hardened. He knew what he had to do, but the weight of his decision loomed over him. It wasn't just about donning a disguise or patrolling the streets; it was about crossing a line from which he could never return. He would be stepping outside the law, risking his reputation, and perhaps even his life. But the cries for justice from the East End, echoing from his past, left him no choice.

That night, Edward began the transformation into The Watcher. In a hidden chamber of Langley Manor, he meticulously crafted his alter ego. He designed a suit that merged functionality with the elegance befitting a man of his station. Beneath the tailored exterior, he concealed lightweight armour, on his face he donned a leather mask that sat on the bridge of his nose and neatly fitted around his pale blue eyes, an elegant high-collared black cloak and hood draped over the midnight blue suit he wore, and his sleek black cane with is ornamental silver raven head handle doubled as a concealed sword. A specially designed grappling hook umbrella completed his ensemble, combining Victorian sophistication with the tools of his nocturnal crusade.

As Edward donned his new persona, he felt a sense of liberation. The Watcher was more than a disguise; he was an embodiment of Edward's deepest convictions. In the privacy of his hidden chamber, Edward practiced with his new tools, each movement bringing him closer to the hero he needed to become.

But with each step into his new role, Edward felt the burden of his double life. He knew his actions would raise suspicions among his peers and potentially place those he cared about in danger. The thought of Mr. Humphrey discovering his secret filled him with unease. Yet, the nobleman's burden was his to bear, and he was resolute in his mission.

As dawn approached, Edward, now The Watcher, stood ready. London's East End, with its labyrinth of shadows and secrets, awaited him. It was time to step out of the shadows of Langley Manor and into the night that cloaked the city.

Chapter 4:

Birth of the Watcher

The moon hung low over London, casting elongated shadows across the cobbled streets of the East End. In the concealed chamber beneath Langley Manor, Edward stood before a mirror, his reflection transformed. The man staring back at him was no longer just a nobleman, but a symbol of justice.

Clad in his meticulously designed attire, Edward felt a surge of purpose. His suit, a harmonious blend of elegance and practicality, was complemented by the armoured underlay that promised protection in the perilous night ahead. His cane, no longer just an accessory of status, was now a weapon of defence, and the grappling hook umbrella at his side, was an ingenious tool for navigating the urban landscape.

Edward took a deep breath, steeling himself for the task ahead. He was about to step into a world far removed from the grand halls of Langley Manor. This was a world where danger lurked in every shadow, a world that cried out for a saviour.

As he made his way through the secret passages of the manor, Edward's mind raced with the plans and strategies he had formulated. He knew the streets of the East End like the back of his hand, the memories of his childhood navigating these very alleys serving him well.

Emerging from the shadows, The Watcher blended into the night. His first destination was Whitechapel, the heart of recent horrors that had shaken the city to its core. As he moved with purpose, his keen eyes surveyed the dimly lit streets, alert to every sound, every movement.

It wasn't long before he encountered the very reality, he had set out to confront. In a narrow alley, the cries of a young woman echoed, her voice filled with terror. Edward's heart raced as he quickened his pace, moving towards the source of the commotion.

He arrived just in time to witness two burley reprobates harassing a lone woman. One man had hold of the woman from behind pulling her arms back so she could not escape while the other armed with a wooden cosh threatened her. Without hesitation, The Watcher intervened. His training, both formal and self-taught, came into play, He rushed forward as he expertly wielded his cane sword, and using a quick downward strike with the flat of the sword he disarmed one of the thugs with swift precision.

The element of surprise was still on his side, in a beat The Watcher delivered a powerful hook with his left hand striking the now-disarmed thug, knocking him to the damp dirty cobbles below. The ruffian who had been holding the woman had now released her as he stood frozen with fear as he watched the black-cloaked vigilante turn his gaze onto him from beneath his hooded mask, the thugs, unprepared for an adversary of his calibre, quickly scattered into the night, leaving their intended victim scared but unharmed.

The woman, still in shock, looked up at her rescuer. "Who are you?" she asked, her eyes wide with a mix of fear and awe. Edward, maintaining his anonymity, simply bowed his head and vanished into the night, leaving the woman to wonder if her saviour was merely a spectre.

As The Watcher continued his patrol, his presence did not go unnoticed. By the end of the night, whispers began to spread among the denizens of the East End. A mysterious figure, a guardian in the night, had emerged. Some dismissed it as a rumour, a tale concocted by the fearful and the hopeful. But for those who had witnessed his intervention, The Watcher was very real.

Meanwhile, back at Langley Manor, Mr. Humphrey noticed the absence of his master. The butler, ever observant, couldn't help but feel a growing concern. Edward's late-night disappearances were becoming more frequent, and the secrecy surrounding them more profound. He pondered whether to confront Edward with his suspicions but ultimately decided against it, trusting that his master had his reasons.

As dawn approached, Edward returned to the Manor, his first night as The Watcher leaving him both exhilarated and burdened. He had stepped into a new world, one that held both danger and the promise of justice. As he retired to his quarters, he knew one thing for certain — his life, and the lives of those in London, would never be the same.

Chapter 5:

The First Dawn

The early morning sun crept through the heavy curtains of Langley Manor, casting a warm glow across the opulent room where Edward sat pensively. The events of the previous night replayed in his mind, the adrenaline of his first intervention as The Watcher still coursing through his veins. The fear in the woman's eyes, the shock and then relief as he intervened and enacted her rescue, lingered with him. He had made a difference, albeit small in the grand tapestry of London's sprawling crime. But it was a start, a step towards the justice he so deeply craved.

Downstairs, Mr. Humphrey noticed the subtle changes in Edward. The dark circles under his eyes spoke of sleepless nights, and there was a new intensity in his demeanour. Concerned, the butler prepared breakfast, contemplating the right words to address his master's evident exhaustion. As Edward descended the stairs, Mr. Humphrey greeted him with a measured expression.

"A good morning to you, sir. I trust you slept well?"

Edward offered a weary smile.

"As well as can be expected, Humphrey. Thank you."

"Are you sure sir? I didn't hear you retire to your chambers last night" Mr Humphrey questioned cautiously.

"I drifted off in my study last night, lost in my thoughts I guess" Edward lied trying not to draw attention to his nightly activity.

"indeed sir" Mr Humphrey nodded, he knew that his master was lying to him but he couldn't fathom why. Knowing better than to press for more answers Mr Humphrey left Edward to his morning meal.

During breakfast, Edward's thoughts were elsewhere. The whispers he had overheard in the alleys and streets of the East End echoed in his mind. The Watcher was already becoming more than just a shadow in the night.

After breakfast, Edward retreated to his study, but his attention was drawn to the latest newspaper headlines. Reports of the mysterious vigilante had started to surface. The story spoke of a cloaked figure who disrupted a robbery, igniting curiosity and hope among the citizens. The police, on the other hand, were less enthusiastic, their statements filled with warnings against vigilante actions.

Edward knew he was treading a delicate line. His actions as The Watcher were already drawing attention, not all of it welcome. He pondered his next move, aware that each night he stepped out, he risked exposing his dual identity, not just to the authorities but to those closest to him.

As night fell, Edward donned his alter ego once more. The weight of the cloak felt comforting, a shield against the world he was about to re-enter. He moved through the city with a new sense of purpose, his senses heightened, his mind alert to every possibility.

His following nights as The Watcher were different. The criminals he encountered were warier, having heard rumours of a guardian in the shadows. Edward found himself not just intervening in crimes but also deterring them, his mere presence enough to make would-be assailants think twice.

But with this new reputation came new challenges. The underworld of London began to take notice, and whispers of a figure in the shadows turned to murmurs of plotting and retaliation. The Watcher was no longer a mere curiosity; he was now a threat to their clandestine activities.

Back at Langley Manor, Mr. Humphrey sat in the dimly lit kitchen, a cup of tea cooling in front of him. He was worried about Edward, more so now with the talk of a vigilante in the newspapers. He knew his master well enough to suspect his involvement, yet he remained silent, his loyalty to Edward overriding his concerns.

As every new dawn broke, Edward returned to his manor, his body weary but his resolve stronger than ever. He knew he had started something that could not be undone, a crusade against the darkness that plagued his city. The Watcher was no longer just a part of him; he was becoming a beacon of hope in a city shrouded in fear.

Chapter 6:

A Legacy of Justice

The day at Langley Manor began like any other, with the grandeur of the estate belying the turmoil that churned beneath its surface. In his study, Edward sat immersed in his thoughts, his eyes tracing over the detailed maps of London spread out before him. These maps were not just guides to the city's streets; they were windows into its soul, revealing the hidden struggles and silent cries for help.

As Edward planned his next move as The Watcher, his mind wandered to the lessons of his father, the late Lord Alexander Langley. These memories, often pushed to the back of his mind, now came flooding forward, offering both guidance and reflection.

Lord Langley had been a man of principle, a beacon of integrity in a society often marred by superficiality and greed. He had instilled in Edward a sense of duty and a deep understanding of the responsibility that came with their privilege.

"We are the stewards of our community, Edward," his father had often said with a deep but kind voice. "Our actions must uplift those who cannot uplift themselves."

These teachings laid the foundation for Edward's transformation into The Watcher. Yet, there was more to his father's legacy than Edward had initially realized. Hidden in the depths of the manor, was a secluded room he had found known only to his father, Months ago Edward had discovered it and the secrets of his father's past – secrets that hinted at a life not unlike the one Edward was now leading.

Journals, newspaper clippings, and notes, carefully preserved, told the story of a man deeply involved in the fight against injustice. Lord Langley had worked in the shadows, using his influence and resources to right wrongs where the law had failed. The Papers had dubbed this man the Guardian, This revelation had shocked Edward at first, but it also provided a newfound sense of connection to his father and a deeper understanding of his path.

As Edward once again reflected on these revelations, Mr. Humphrey entered the study with a tray of tea. The butler's gaze lingered on the maps and clippings of the stories of the Guardian strewn across the desk, his expression betraying a hint of concern.

"What are these sir?" Mr. Humphrey asked.

"News clippings, I found them with my father's effects" Edward stated without looking up. "He seemed to have an interest in the crimes of the East End, much like me" he continued

"Your father did much to help the poor an desolate sir" Mr. Humphrey said proudly.

"I know he did Humphrey, I just hope I can live up to his legacy" Edward said solemnly.

"Your father would be proud of the man you've become, sir," Mr. Humphrey remarked, placing his hand gently on his masters shoulder.

Edward looked up, a faint smile on his lips.

"Thank you, Humphrey I hope you are right."

That night, as Edward roamed the streets as The Watcher, his father's teachings echoed in his mind. Each intervention, each act of protection, was a tribute to the legacy The Guardian had left behind. Edward was no longer just fighting for justice; he was continuing a family tradition, one that transcended generations.

The East End, with its dark alleys and hidden dangers, had now become The Watcher's domain. His presence was now felt, not just by those he saved, but by those who lurked in the shadows, their nefarious deeds disrupted by his actions.

However, with increased recognition came increased risk. Edward knew that his alter ego was drawing the attention of more than just common criminals. The police, too, were taking an interest in The Watcher, their initial scepticism turning into a resolve to uncover the identity of the mysterious vigilante.

As the first light of dawn touched the horizon, Edward again returned to Langley Manor, his body tired but his spirit undeterred. He was no longer just Edward Langley, a nobleman, and heir to a legacy of wealth. He was The Watcher, heir to a legacy of justice, and his journey had only just begun.

Chapter 7:

Shadows of Whitechapel

The evening air in London was brisk, carrying with it whispers of the unknown and unspoken fears. In his study at Langley Manor, Edward was deeply engrossed in a collection of reports and maps. The infamous Whitechapel murders, gruesome and unsolved, were spreading terror throughout London. Edward felt a deep, compelling urge to delve into this mystery.

His study was a sanctuary of sorts, lined with books and illuminated by the soft glow of a solitary lamp. Here, Edward felt the weight of his dual identity, torn between the world of aristocracy and the shadowy realm of vigilantism. The latest reports on the Ripper case were scattered before him, the most recent murder of Annie Chapman had shocked the city, each detail a piece of an enigmatic puzzle that eluded even Scotland Yard's finest.

As Edward pored over the reports, Mr. Humphrey entered, carrying a silver tray with a pot of tea. The butler's eyes briefly scanned the scattered papers, a silent acknowledgment of his master's obsession.

"Will you be attending Lady Harrow's birthday celebrations tomorrow, sir?" Mr. Humphrey inquired, setting down the tray.

Edward looked up, momentarily distracted, as a small smile spread across his face. The thought of seeing Eleanor Harrow always cheered him up and over the years he had become quite fond of her, maybe more than he was comfortable to admit.

"Ah, yes, the party. I had almost forgotten. Yes, Humphrey, I will attend."

Mr. Humphrey nodded, aware that such social obligations were now more of an afterthought for Edward.

"Very good, sir. I shall have your suit prepared." Mr. Humphrey responded and he turned and left the study gently closing the door behind him.

Left alone once more, Edward's thoughts returned to the Ripper case. The brutality of the murders, the fear they instigated, and the mystery surrounding the killer's identity drew a parallel with his crusade against injustice. He felt a growing responsibility to involve The Watcher in the hunt for this elusive predator.

That night, as The Watcher patrolled the labyrinthine streets of Whitechapel, the sense of danger was palpable. The fog seemed to carry the echoes of unspeakable horrors, and every shadow appeared to conceal lurking threats.

As he moved through the dark alleys, he encountered not just the common criminals of London's underworld but also the palpable fear of its citizens. Whispers of "The Ripper" filled the air, a name that had become synonymous with terror. The Watcher's presence offered a fleeting sense of security, a brief respite from the pervasive dread.

In the dim light of a gas lamp, Edward came across a piece of bloodied cloth, it looked to be from a cotton apron or blouse, Edward immediately thought of the recent newspaper he read about the Ripper's letters designed to taunt the city's efforts to catch the killer. He studied it carefully, committing every detail to memory. Was it a clue? However small, every clue brought him closer to understanding the mind behind the murders.

As dawn approached, Edward returned to his sanctuary, his thoughts swirling with the complexities of the case. He knew that his involvement as The Watcher was a risk, but it was one he was willing to take. The streets of Whitechapel needed a protector, and he was determined to be that beacon of hope amidst the darkness.

Chapter 8:

The Lady

The following morning Edward wearily arose from bed. As he looked to his bedside table, he saw that the ever-faithful Mr. Humphrey had already prepared his breakfast and left the daily issue of the Globe paper. Edward's eye was immediately drawn to an article about one of the Ripper's most recent victims, Annie Chapman. The article was about the funeral on the 14th of September, now the 29th the Globe had rightly or wrongly decided to share the details with the public. The article read;

"The utmost secrecy was observed in the arrangements, and none but the undertaker, the police, and the relatives of the deceased knew anything about it.

Shortly after seven o'clock, a hearse drew up outside the mortuary in Montagu-street and the body was quickly removed.

At nine o'clock a start was made for Manor Park Cemetery, the place selected by the friends of the deceased for the interment, but no coaches followed, as it was desired that public attention should not be attracted.

Mr. Smith and other relatives met the body at the cemetery, and the service was duly performed in the ordinary manner.

The remains of the deceased were enclosed in a black covered elm coffin, which bore the words, "Annie Chapman, died September 8, 1888, aged 48 years."

As Edward read these words to himself a wave of sadness, anger, and frustration washed over him. He thought to himself about how he may have been able to stop the tragedy had he been there, although at the date of her death at the beginning of September, he had yet to assume the mantle of The Watcher. His deep thoughts were interrupted suddenly by Mr. Humphrey who had entered the chambers with a quick knock on the door.

"Good morning, Sir," he said with a kind smile "I was beginning to fear you would sleep the whole day".

Edward with a start grabbed at the clock on the bedside table, it's delicate hands indicating it was almost midday.

"Blast!" Edward exclaimed as he shot out of bed throwing the fine cotton sheets to the floor. "I shall be late for Lady Harrow's Birthday celebrations".

"Fear not sir," Mr Humphreys said calmly. "The carriage is prepared, the horses ready and I have sent word of our late arrival."

"Thank you, Humphrey," Edward said as he franticly dressed himself in the fine suit that Mr Humphrey had already laid out for him while he slumbered. "How would I manage without you?"

"How indeed sir, How Indeed," Mr. Humphrey said as he left the bed chambers.

The Carriage ride from Westminster to Paddington was uneventful and gave Edward time to reflect on his work as The Watcher, as he looked out at the affluent West End he pondered over the contrasting sides of the city. His efforts thus far were on the violent crimes of the East End, but he was not naive enough to believe that the corruption of crime was not present on his very doorstep.

It wasn't long before Edward was walking up the steps of the Harrow estate. He was greeted at the door by the house staff who took his cloak and handed him a flute of sparkling wine. He was led to the main hall where he was met with crowds of the well-dressed and well-off members of London's society. As Edward scanned the room he saw many familiar faces of public figures, politicians, officials, tycoons, and business owners. Edward wondered if anyone here other than himself was actually a friend of Lady Harrow. As Edward made his way through the crowd, he overheard conversations about mundane policies, politics, and finance. Edward was no stranger to high society and these sorts of events, although he had great disdain for them, he knew how to act and what to say. He made idle talk and nodded politely, now and again he would hear talk of the vigilante seen in the East End, but most people of this class dismissed it as rumour or fiction, a story created by the poor to make their lives more interesting and their existence less bleak. Edward navigated the sea of aristocrats with practiced ease, his charming demeanour belying the inner turmoil of his dual life. It was here that he encountered Inspector Frederick Abberline, the lead inspector on the Ripper case, who was in attendance to garner support for the police's efforts in Whitechapel.

"Mr. Langley, a pleasure to see you," Inspector Abberline greeted, extending his hand.

"The pleasure is mine, Inspector," Edward replied, shaking his hand. "I trust your efforts in Whitechapel are progressing?"

Abberline's expression darkened slightly. "It's a challenging case, Mr. Langley. The killer is elusive, and now we have this vigilante, The Watcher the people are calling him, it's complicating matters."

Edward maintained his composure, his interest apparent. "Indeed, the city is abuzz with talk of this Watcher. But is he not aiding your cause, in a way?"

Abberline sighed. "Perhaps, but vigilantism is a dangerous path. We cannot condone individuals taking the law into their own hands."

As their conversation continued, it felt like a delicate dance of words and opinions. Edward carefully navigated the discussion, offering support while concealing his true involvement. As the discussion came to a polite and natural end, Edward continued to make his way through the crowd, his mind racing with the implications of his conversation with Abberline. The Watcher's role in the city was becoming increasingly complex, and the line between ally and adversary was blurring.

It felt like a lifetime passed before Edward finally found her in the crowd, Lady Eleanor Harrow. Edward's eyes locked on her as she walked towards him in her flowing ball gown, her jet-black hair perfectly styled for the event with not a strand out of place and her emerald eyes smiled as she saw him.

"Mr. Langley," She said as she curtsied "I'm so glad that you decided to attend".

"I wouldn't have missed it for the world Lady Harrow" He responded as he took her hand a gently kissed it.

"Well, you were late" she smirked. Edward blushed like a child.

"fashionably" he retorted. Trying to compose himself. There was something about Eleanor that caused Edward's heart to race. Perhaps it was her beauty or perhaps it was the simple fact that like himself there was something about her that didn't fit within these high society events, she always had a look of mischief and adventure in her eyes and her unpredictability both frightened and excited Edward in equal measure. For the rest of the afternoon and long into the evening Edward and Eleanor were at each other's side, laughing, drinking, and talking. The Party guests had begun to leave as the event had wound down and for just one day Edward had managed to forget about the crime-riddled streets of the east end and was able to enjoy the company of a woman who had a powerful effect on his heart.

"Oh Edward, I have had such a wonderful time with you today, why must it always be so long between your visits?" Eleanor questioned as she walked him to the door where his carriage was waiting to take him home.

"I am sorry Eleanor, I have been preoccupied as of late, sorting the estate, I still have a large amount of my father's affairs to get in order," Edward said solemnly, it wasn't entirely a lie, but he knew he couldn't tell her the truth, even though he desperately wanted to.

"Your father, of course how could I forget. How selfish of me, I was very sad to hear of his passing he was always so kind to me" Eleanor said as the smile faded from her face.

"Not selfish at all, you had more pressing things to worry about today, mainly avoiding getting embroiled in a political debate or a lecture on the economy" Edward smirked "How many of the guests did you know?"

"Not many" Eleanor smiled back "They are mainly my father's associates".

"How is Lord Harrow nowadays?" Edward asked as they reached the front door "I didn't see him today".

"He is always busy with his imports and exports, he owns so many of the warehouses on the docks now, he might as well move his estate there," she said sarcastically. "He was here today for a time, but was called away, he often has to see to business in the evenings" Eleanor continued with sadness in her voice. "Honestly it is beyond me why he must see to issues himself".

"I'm sure he wouldn't have gone if he didn't have to," Edward said reassuringly "Speaking of which, it is late, I too must be going, Happy Birthday Lady Harrow" as Edward turned to leave Eleanor quickly and gently pecked him on the cheek. Edward immediately flushed red once again.

"Farewell Mr Langley," she said through her mischievous smile.

When Edward returned to Langley manor he retired to his chambers. A smile on his face as he fell asleep, he thought to himself about his night with Eleanor. A well-deserved night off from being the Watcher.

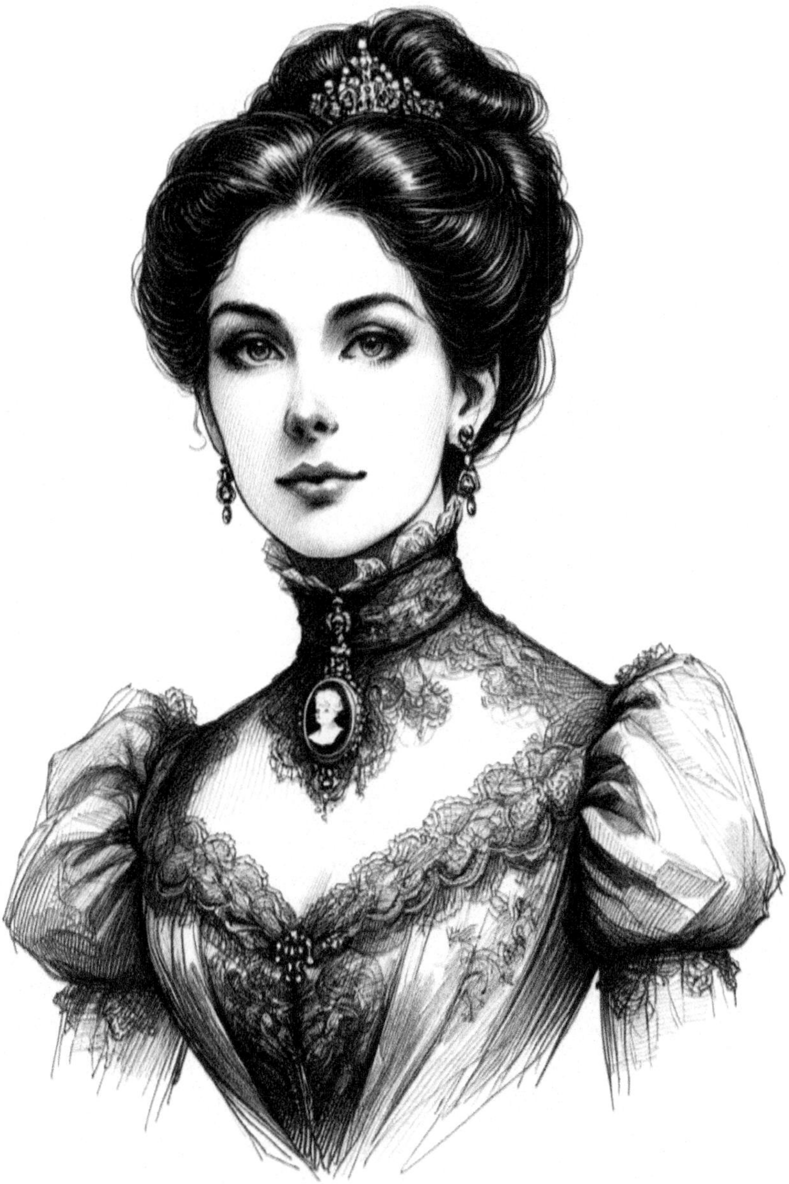

Chapter 9:

Conflicted Alliances

The morning sunbathed Langley Manor in a warm, golden light, a stark contrast to the darkness that Edward had been encountering in the streets of Whitechapel as of late. As he sat in his study, well-rested after a night off from his nocturnal endeavours, his determination remained unshaken.

Edward picked up the morning issue of The Globe that Mr. Humprey had once again left for him. As Edward read the front page his blood ran cold.

"THE RIPPER STRIKES AGAIN!"

He furiously read the article; *"In the early morning hours of this very morning, Sunday 30th September 1888. The body of Elizabeth Stride was discovered at approximately one o'clock in Dutfield's Yard, off Berner Street in Whitechapel. The cause of death was a single clear-cut incision, measuring six inches across her neck which had severed from her left before terminating beneath her right jaw. The absence of any further mutilations to her body has led to uncertainty within Scotland Yard as to whether Stride's murder was committed by the Ripper, or whether he was merely interrupted during the attack. Several witnesses later informed the police they had seen Stride in the company of a man in or close to Berner Street on the evening of the 29th. September and in the early hours of 30th September, but each gave inconsistent descriptions.*

Just three-quarters of an hour after the discovery of the body of Elizabeth Stride another body was found in a corner of Mitre Square in the City of London, this was the body of Catherine Eddowes, her throat was severed from ear to ear and her abdomen ripped open, a long, deep and jagged wound. Her intestines had been placed over her right shoulder, with a section of intestine being completely detached and placed between her body and left arm."

Edward felt sick, his blood ran cold. While he was drinking and dining with high society, The infamous Ripper had taken another two lives, he should have been there, he should have stopped it. He had no excuses, and the guilt was consuming him. Edward spent the day solemn and depressed, the merriment and joy of the previous day forgotten like a distant memory. As dusk drew near, he donned his Watcher ensemble and headed off into the night to atone for his perceived failings.

The Watcher's first stop was Dutfield's Yard. The recent developments in the Whitechapel murders had not only heightened the sense of fear in London but had also drawn increased attention from Scotland Yard. The police were now under immense pressure to capture the infamous Jack the Ripper, and their frustration was growing with each unsuccessful attempt. It was clear to Edward that the police patrols in Whitechapel had increased substantially.

Moving through the shadows Edward quickly and quietly made his way through the wooden gate of the yard to the spot where Elizabeth Stride had met her brutal end. The Yard was dark with almost no light reaching the area from the gas lamps on the street. Edward pulled a match from a pouch on his belt and struck it on the wall. As the match flame burst to life he held it close to the floor where Stride had been found but it was quickly apparent to him that any chances of a clue from this location were almost non-existent. The ground was muddy and wet. The police had walked over the whole scene, and it was impossible for Edward to deduce if any footprints here belonged to the killer. Once again Edward was pained with guilt. The Watcher should have been here last night, not at some party.

Edward accepting that all evidence here was lost snuck back out of the yards and made his way to Mitre Square. This location was still abuzz with police officers. Realizing that he couldn't get close to the spot where Catherine Eddowes had been found Edward made his way to a rooftop that overlooked the square and surveyed the area from above. The amount of police with their lanterns had lit the square adequately. It wasn't long before Edward saw Inspector Abberline on the scene talking to officers and giving instructions. From Edward's location he was unable to hear what was being said among the officers and opted to get closer. As Edward lowered himself onto a slightly lower roof he slipped, and a slate shingle detached from the roof and smashed on the cobbles below. Lantern beams illuminated the Watcher and Police whistles screeched.

"YOU THERE!" an officer bellowed

"STOP IN THE NAME OF THE LAW!" another ordered.

Edward had to think quickly, he dropped onto the lower roof and snatched an item from a pouch on his belt. He hurled it at the floor at the officer's feet. It shattered and smoke plumed out quickly filling the square. As the police coughed and spluttered The Watcher disappeared into the night.

It was now apparent that amidst London's turmoil, The Watcher's presence in the city had not gone unnoticed by the authorities. After tonight's events, Edward knew that Inspector Frederick Abberline would begin to take more of an interest in the mysterious vigilante. However, Edward hoped that the Inspector's views were a mix of scepticism and reluctant admiration. He knew that Abberline disapproved of vigilante justice, but Edward knew he couldn't deny the effectiveness of The Watcher's interventions.

Edward, knew he had to tread carefully. His actions as The Watcher were meant to aid the city, not to create additional conflict. However, he also understood that his methods, operating outside the law, would inevitably lead to clashes with the authorities.

This delicate balance was further complicated by Edward's social standing. As a respected nobleman, he had connections and influence within the very institutions that sought to uncover The Watcher's identity. His attendance at social events, such as Lady Harrow's party had put him in close proximity to those who might be instrumental in his downfall. The Watcher continued his patrol through the night, stopping as many crimes as he could however staying as far from the police as he could at all times.

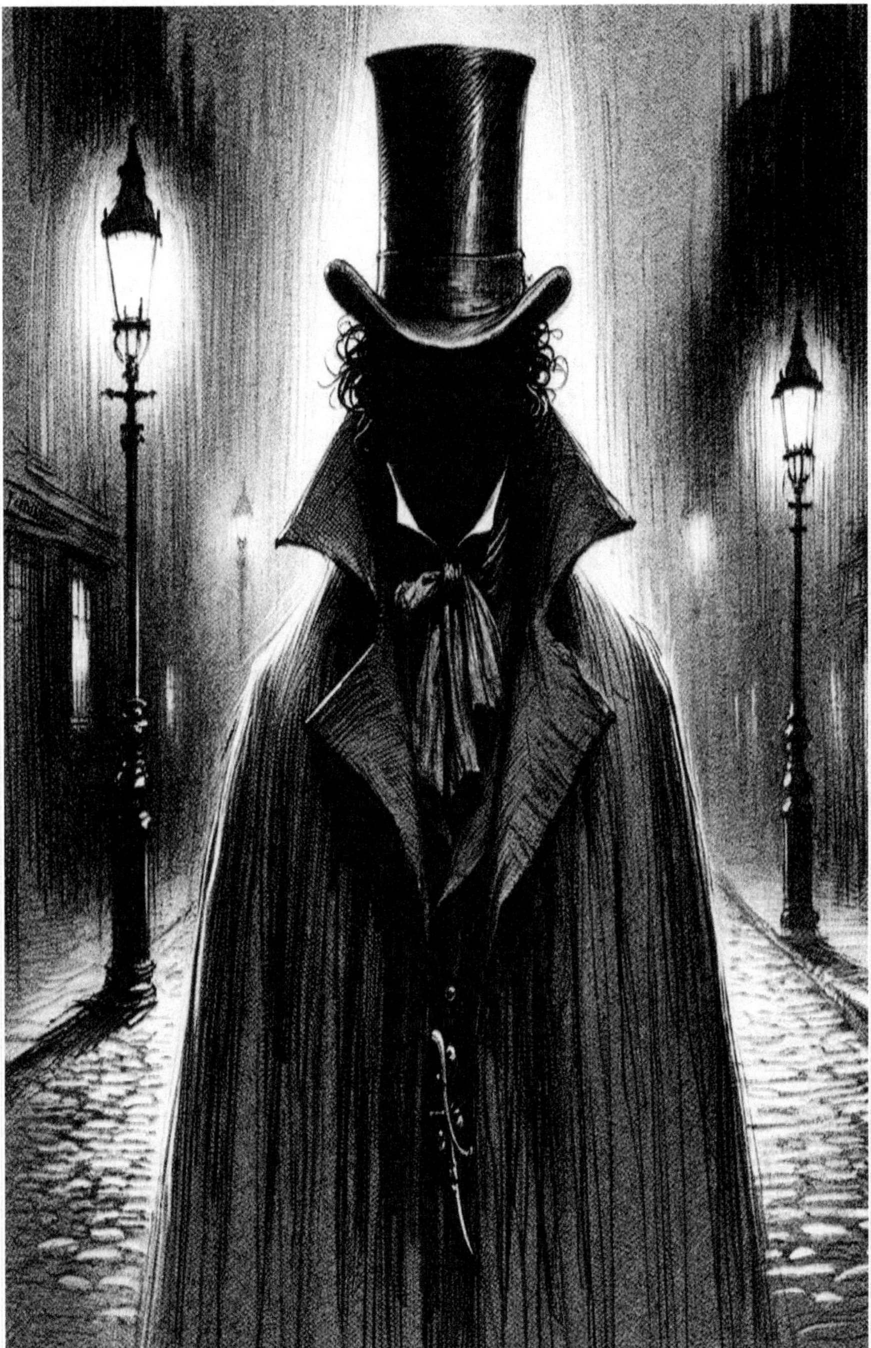

Chapter 10:

The Hidden Sanctuary

The evening shadows lengthened over Langley Manor, casting a serene stillness that belied the turbulence within its master's heart. In the depths of the estate, hidden from the world, lay Edward's secret sanctuary, his father's hidden room – a place where The Watcher was forged. This hidden chamber was where Edward honed his skills and strategized his next moves.

The room was a stark contrast to the rest of the manor, functional and austere. Walls lined with maps and clippings formed a tapestry of London's underworld. A workbench held various tools and gadgets, each serving a purpose in Edward's crusade. In one corner, The Watcher's suit hung, a symbol of the oath Edward had taken to protect the innocent.

Edward sat at his desk, his eyes intently studying a map of Whitechapel. The recent encounters and the information gleaned from them had started to form a pattern. He plotted points on the map, each representing a clue, a sighting, a piece of the puzzle that was Jack the Ripper. Despite the danger, Edward knew that The Watcher's involvement was crucial. He could move in ways the police could not, probing into the shadows where the true face of evil often lurked.

Edward returned to his study upstairs and as he delved deeper into his planning, he was interrupted by the sound of a discreet knock at the door. He called out for the visitor to enter. Mr. Humphrey stepped in, his expression a mix of concern and respect.

"Sir, you've been secluded for hours. Might I bring you something to eat?" Mr. Humphrey asked, his eyes glancing around the room, aware that there was more to his master's activities than met the eye.

Edward, realizing the toll his secret life was taking on his old friend, offered a reassuring smile. "Thank you, Humphrey, but I'm quite alright. Just some mundane matters to attend to."

Mr. Humphrey nodded, understanding the boundaries of his position. Yet his worry for Edward was palpable. "Very well, sir. Do call if you need anything." He said and once again retreated from his master's study.

Left alone again, Edward's mind returned to the task at hand. The responsibility he bore as The Watcher weighed heavily on him. Each night he ventured into the city, he walked a fine line between hero and outlaw, a line that became more blurred with each passing day.

That night, as he donned The Watcher's suit, Edward felt a renewed sense of purpose. The hidden sanctuary had served, not just as a place of preparation but as a reminder of the commitment he had made to himself, his father, and London.

The Watcher's presence in Whitechapel had become a beacon of hope for some and a threat to others. As he moved through the foggy streets, Edward was acutely aware of the many eyes that followed him – some filled with gratitude, others with malice.

In the dark alleys and hidden corners of the city, Edward continued his search for clues, each step bringing him closer to the heart of the darkness that plagued Whitechapel. He knew that the path he walked was fraught with danger, but he was driven by a duty that transcended fear.

As dawn approached, The Watcher disappeared into the shadows, returning to the sanctuary beneath Langley Manor. Edward would resume his public façade, but the echoes of the night lingered, a constant reminder of the dual life he led.

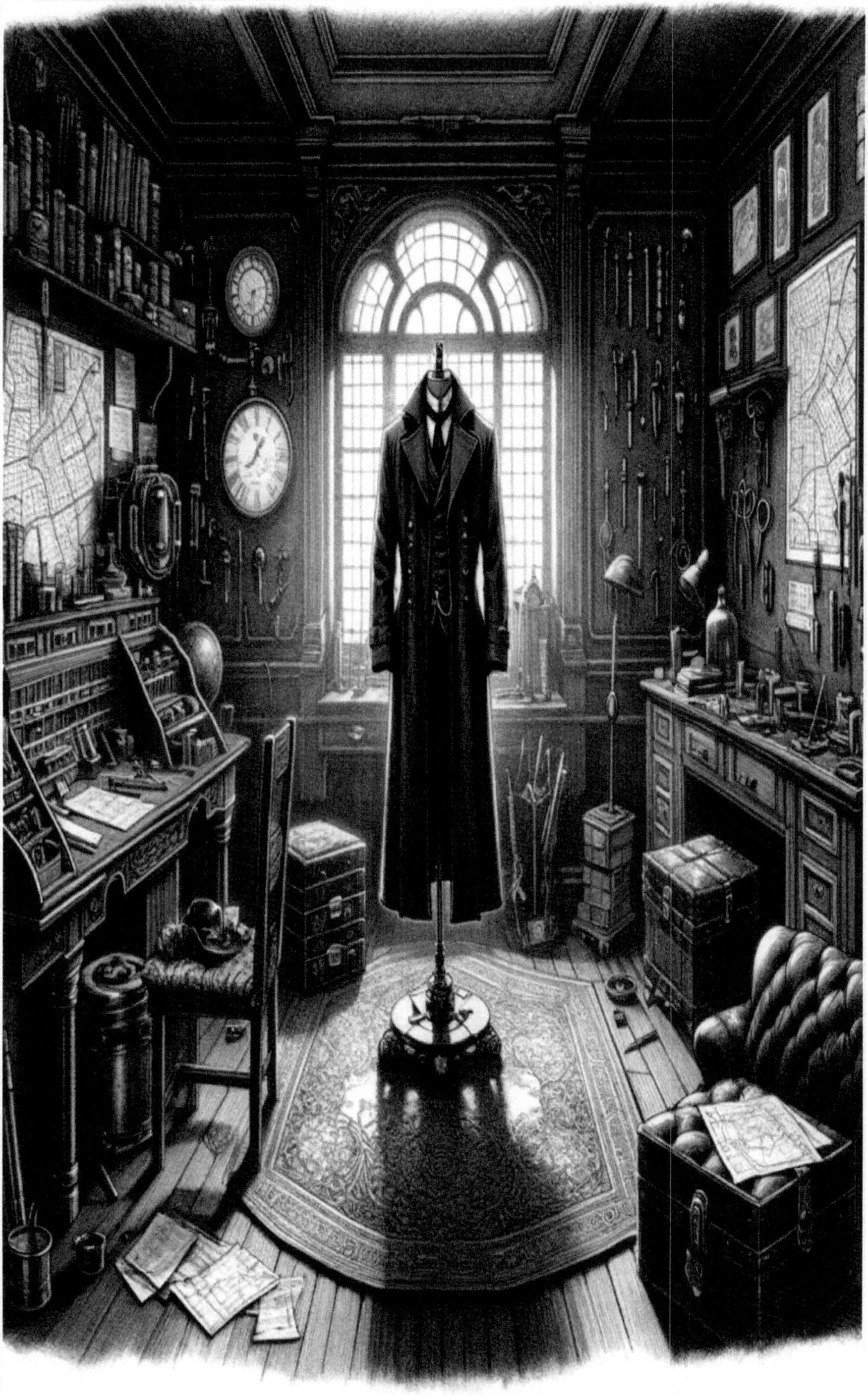

Chapter 11:

A Darker Turn

The rising sun marked the end of another night's patrol, a routine that had become both a calling and a curse. In his hidden chamber, Edward reflected on the events of the past few weeks. His dual life was becoming increasingly challenging to manage. As The Watcher, he had started to make a difference, but the weight of his secret identity was taking a toll, both physically and mentally.

This morning, Edward's contemplation was disrupted by an unexpected development. Mr. Humphrey, with a look of grave concern, presented Edward with a letter delivered directly to Langley Manor. The seal was unfamiliar, a stark red wax with no discernible print. Edward opened the letter cautiously. Inside, he found a message that sent a chill down his spine. The scrawling letter penned in red ink read;

"Dear old Watcher, or should I call you Eddie?

I keep hearing people say you will catch me, but you and the police won't fix me just yet. I have a laugh when they walk past me on the cobbles, none the wiser it gives me real fits.

I doubled down on whores last time and I shan't quit ripping them till I do get buckled. Number one squealed, couldn't finish straight off, Grand work the last job was, I gave the lady no time to squeal.

How can <u>YOU</u> catch me, if the world finds out <u>YOUR</u> little secret? Can you stop my work before I tell?

I love my work and want to start again. You will soon hear more of me with my funny little games. I saved some of the proper red stuff in a ginger beer bottle after the first job to write with, but it went thick like glue, and I can't use it. Red ink is fit enough I hope. The next job I do I shall do a real nasty, my knife's so nice and sharp I want to get to work right away if I get a chance. Good Luck.

Yours truly

Jack the Ripper"

It was a direct challenge, a taunting provocation from someone who knows of The Watcher's true identity. The Ripper has knowledge of Edward's nightly activities and proposes a sinister game of cat and mouse in the shadows of London.

The implications were alarming. The Ripper had not only discovered his secret but was now threatening to expose him. Edward was now truly realizing that the Ripper was no ordinary criminal; they were cunning, resourceful, and, most worryingly, they held the power to unravel his life as both Edward Langley and The Watcher.

Edward knew he had to tread carefully. This was a game with high stakes, one that required a blend of his aristocratic influence and his vigilante skills to navigate. He decided to use the resources at his disposal to double his efforts.

That night, The Watcher, scoured the streets of Whitechapel, searching for any clue that might lead him to his antagonist. He visited all of the Ripper crime scenes and spent hours meticulously looking for clues and patterns. His investigation took him deeper into the underbelly of London, where whispers in the criminal underworld spoke of a city shrouded in mystery and fear.

As he delved further, The watcher began to look for a pattern emerging in the crimes, were their locations and timing as random as he first thought, could it be possible that the Ripper was a mastermind, striking from the shadows, while manipulating both the criminal world and the aristocracy. Edward had many questions but little to no answers.

In one of the dimly lit alleys, The Watcher saw a glimpse of something pinned to a fence, as he walked closer he could see it was a folded piece of paper with stains of red ink on the edge. He pulled it down and opened it.

"*I'm watching the watcher*" was scrawled in the same red handwriting as before. He was here Edward thought to himself he's been watching me the whole time. This encounter left him once again with more questions than answers, but it also steeled his resolve. He understood that this was no longer just a battle for justice; it was a personal war for survival.

As the first light of dawn crept over the horizon, Edward returned to Langley Manor, his mind racing with the night's revelations. The challenge he faced was daunting, but he was determined to protect his identity and continue his mission. Edward couldn't shake the feeling that he was being watched, that he was stepping into a trap set by an enemy who was always one step ahead.

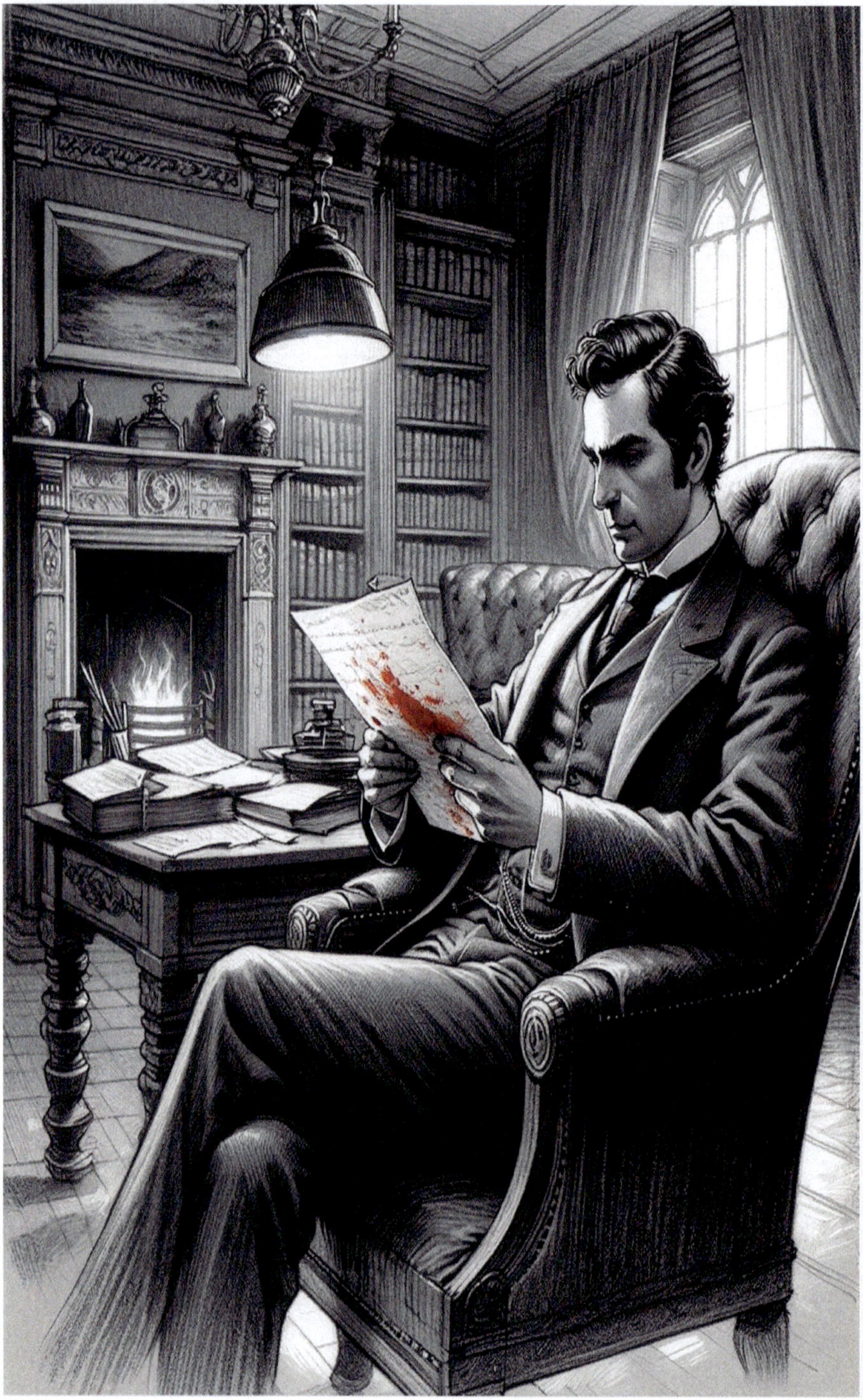

Chapter 12:

Collision Course

The morning light filtered through the stained-glass windows of Langley Manor, casting a kaleidoscope of colours across the grand hall. In the quiet of his study, Edward pondered his next move. It had been days since The Rippers letter and its implications had set in motion a dangerous game, one that threatened to expose Edward's dual existence.

The challenge posed by The Ripper forced Edward to delve deeper into both the high society of London and its shadowy underbelly. He had begun to investigate killings that had not officially been attributed to The Ripper but had minor similarities, some dating back years, Edward began to think he was seeing a pattern but was still not completely sure. During the days he attended social gatherings, his demeanour calm and composed, all the while gathering information, looking for any hint or clue that might lead him to the Ripper.

As The Watcher, Edward's nights were spent patrolling the streets with increased vigilance. The note in the alley had been a stark reminder of the risks he faced. His interactions with the denizens of the night – from informants to petty criminals – became more strategic, as he sought to uncover the identity of his foe. Meanwhile, the city of London buzzed with rumours and speculation. The Watcher's presence had become a topic of conversation across all strata of society, from the smoky taverns of the East End to the opulent drawing rooms of the West End. Edward's efforts to maintain the balance between his two identities grew more challenging with each passing day.

One evening, Edward attended a lavish ball hosted by the Duke of Wellington, who was by all accounts one of the fattest men Edward had ever seen, his booming voice could be heard Echoing from any corner of the grand hall where the ball was taking place. Due to this, it wasn't long before Edward's attention was caught by a conversation between the Duke and a group of influential guests. They spoke in semi-hushed tones about The Ripper.

"The streets of the East End have never been safe," one guest said dismissively.

"Additionally, he is only killing harlots and those of ill repute" a second added. "he's fighting crime, Queen Victoria should knight the man" he added with a pretentious chuckle.

The group laughed as the Duke spoke with as much a hushed tone as he could manage "Well I hear that he may be closer to our social circles than we think, my tailor claims to have recently made a cloak for a man who told him that he had met another man who claimed to be the Ripper, That very cloak was intended for the Ripper, allegedly"

As Edward listened close by, he wondered, if this monstrous killer might have been living in both the criminal underworld and the upper echelons of society. The information resonated with Edward. He had heard it whispered in the alleys of Whitechapel and now in the halls of power. It seemed that his adversary had a reach far beyond what he had initially anticipated.

 This Ripper was more than just a criminal; they were a master strategist, manipulating events for their unknown purposes. With ties to the highest society members and possibly even Dukes and Royalty. Armed with this new information, Edward intensified his investigation. Each piece of information was a potential lead, each encounter a chance to learn more about the man behind the Ripper persona. The Watcher's presence in the city's darker corners became more pronounced, his actions more deliberate. But with each move Edward made, it seemed that his foe was always a step ahead. A mysterious figure shadowed his movements, it was as if his adversary was anticipating his every move, playing a game of chess where The Watcher was perpetually in check.

Despite the mounting challenges, Edward's resolve did not waver. He knew that he must outsmart his enemy, the enemy of the people of his city, and unravel the web of intrigue and deceit that had been woven around him. The safety of his identity and the future of his mission as The Watcher depended on it.

As dawn broke once again over the city, Edward returned to the manor, his mind a whirlwind of thoughts and strategies. The game with The Ripper was reaching a critical point, and he knew that the next move could be the deciding one. Each moment was fraught with danger and uncertainty, two shadows in the night, were on a collision course but The Watcher was ready to face whatever challenges lay ahead.

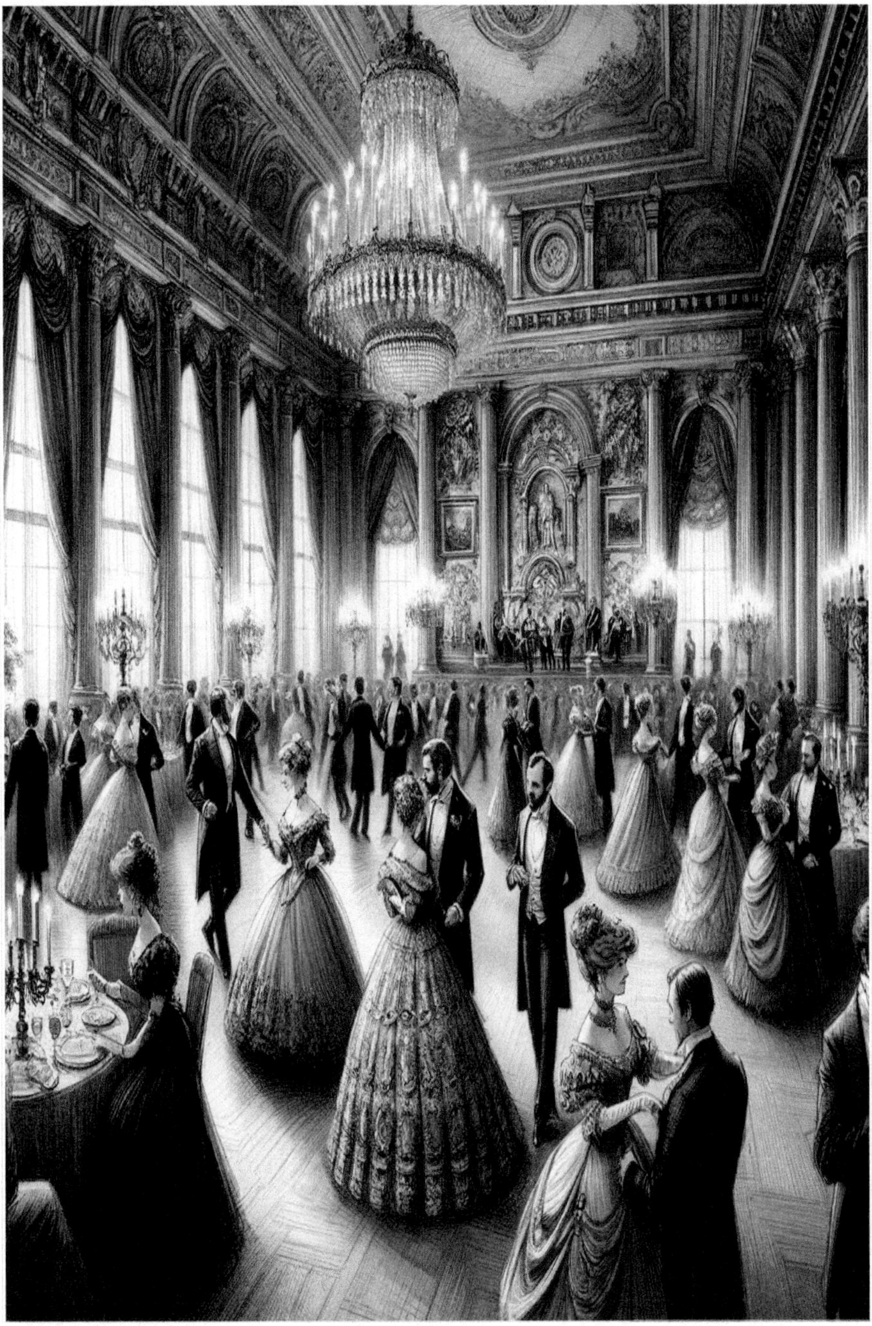

Chapter 13:

The Watcher and the Ripper

The relentless passage of time in London brought with it an air of unease. The streets, once bustling with life, now whispered with secrets and fear, especially in the shadowed corners of Whitechapel. Edward, under the guise of The Watcher, found himself increasingly entwined in the city's darker narratives, his every move watched and countered by the deadly Ripper.

In his hidden chamber beneath Langley Manor, Edward studied the reports of the Ripper murders once again. The gruesome details of the killings sent a shiver down his spine, a grim reminder of the brutality that lurked within the human soul. It wasn't just the savagery of the murders that troubled him, but the elusiveness of the killer, a spectre that seemed to vanish into the foggy night with each heinous act.

The streets of Whitechapel had become a chessboard, with each player moving in the shadows, their intentions obscured by a veil of mystery.

One night not long before dawn, The Watcher patrolled the labyrinthine alleys. As he reached Millers Court off Dorset Street, he came across a crime scene. The police, along with Inspector Abberline, were gathered, their faces etched with frustration and despair. Edward lingered in the shadows, watching, listening. The Ripper had struck again, leaving behind a trail of horror and a city gripped by fear.

As Edward continued his investigation, he looked for patterns, subtle connections that hinted at a larger, more sinister plot that seemed to align with the Ripper's strikes, as if the murders were part of a grand, twisted strategy but found none.

Determined to uncover the truth, Edward delved deeper into the crime scene. Using his agility and stealth he slipped by the constables unnoticed and entered 13 Miller's Court but what greeted him inside was something he would never be able to forget.

An extensively mutilated and disembowelled body of a woman was lying on the bed in the small single room, her face had been hacked beyond all recognition, her throat severed down to the spine, and the abdomen almost emptied of its organs. The organs had been placed beneath her head, and other viscera from her body placed beside her foot, about the bed, and sections of her abdomen and thighs upon a bedside table. Edward felt as if he was about to be sick, but he knew that he had to find a clue, something to point him toward the Ripper or his Identity. He scanned the room thoroughly, the fireplace had not long been extinguished the flames had been hot, so hot in fact that it had melted the spout off the kettle that now lay in the grate. Next to the fireplace however was a small partially burnt scrap of paper. The Watcher quickly seized it, opening it up as he read, he saw it was a list of street names written in black ink but in handwriting that The Watcher recognised, the same scrawling handwriting of The Ripper, the note read;

"Green Street

Ellen Street

Church street

Mansell Street"

Edward quickly tucked it into his cloak and slipped unnoticed back out onto the streets. To find a safe spot to begin to analyse the potential clue he had discovered.

Meanwhile, on the streets, The police were discussing the murder and speculation was spreading, their perception of The Watcher began to shift. Once seen as a shadowy vigilante, doubts and questions arose. Under pressure to solve the Ripper case, they were viewing The Watcher with suspicion, wondering if he was somehow connected to the ongoing atrocities was this vigilante also Jack the Ripper.

Edward felt the walls closing in, the challenges he faced becoming more complex and perilous. But his commitment to justice never wavered. He knew that he must find the Ripper and expose him before more lives were lost and his own identity was revealed.

As the night drew to an end, The Watcher analysed his clue, he quickly noticed that the streets noted on the list were all in close proximity to murder sights, all except one, there had been no murder near Mansell Street, but it was too far for the Watcher to get to before dawn. He quickly went to the nearest address on the list that he found, Church Street.

As he searched the alley that ran parallel to the road, he discovered a critical clue a symbol on the wall in red ink. Searching the bricks, he discovered it to be partially false, disguising a hidden room in an abandoned building. Inside it looked as if it had been used recently, very recently, an extinguished candle had warm wet wax still dripping down its side, had the Ripper just left here? Edward thought to himself or was he still here, on the ground was what appeared to be a black leather bag not dissimilar to those carried by physicians, The Watcher opened the bag only to find it empty, but the fabric interior was ruined and stained with blood. It was a revelation that changed everything, a connection that brought clarity and focus to his mission, The Ripper is using safe houses, possibly to hide before and after crimes and his next victim will be near Mansell Street unless the Watcher can stop him first.

As he left the building, Edward knew that the final confrontation was imminent. The Watcher and the Ripper, only one could emerge victorious.

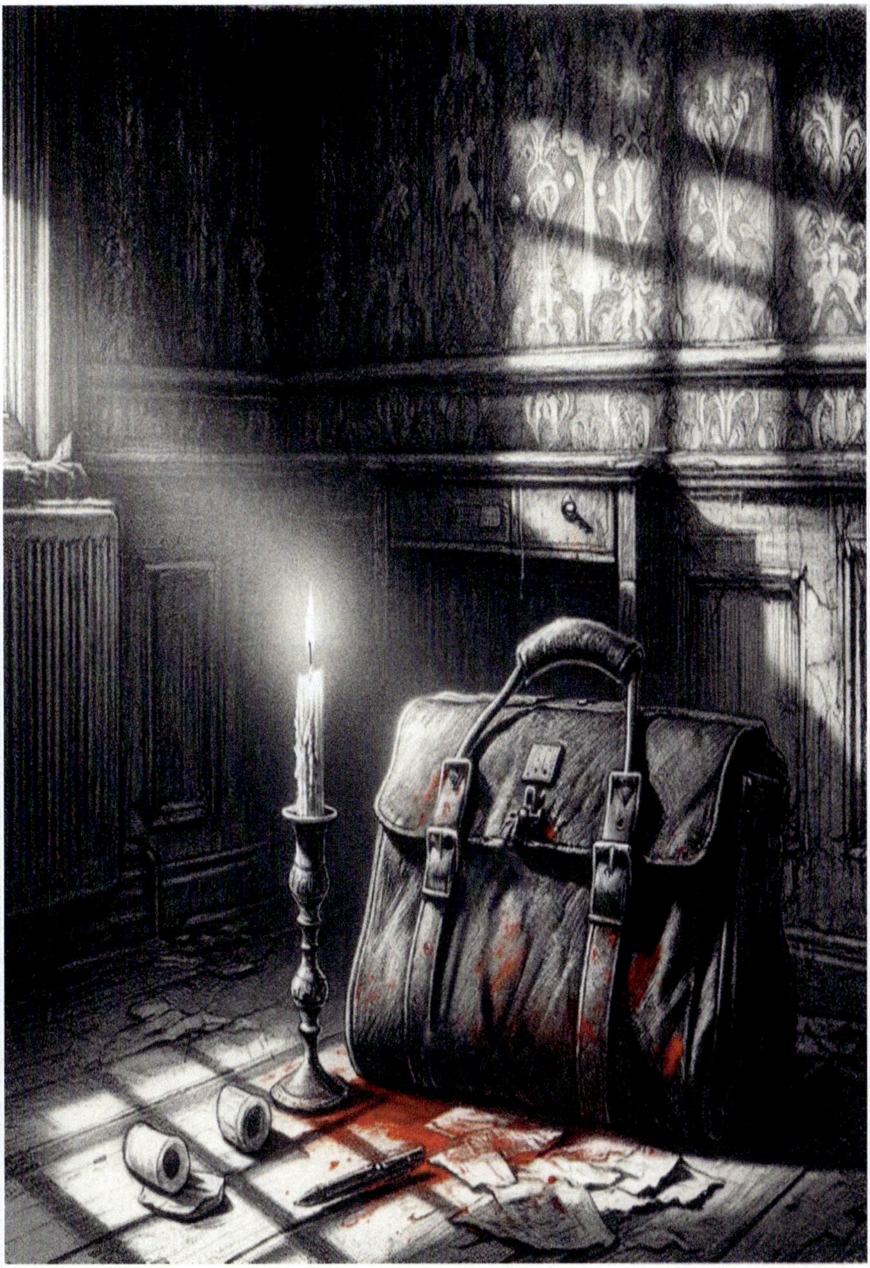

Chapter 14:
The Night's End

This night in London had a different quality, a tension that hung in the air like a thick fog. Edward felt this tension acutely as he prepared for what he knew would be a pivotal confrontation. The Ripper who had cast a dark shadow over the city was about to be brought into light.

In his hidden chamber beneath Langley Manor, Edward reviewed the evidence once more. The link between the Ripper murders and the potential safe houses was undeniable, and he knew that the next few hours could change the course of London's history. Donning his cloak and mask, he set out into the night with a sense of purpose that bordered on the obsessive.

The streets of Whitechapel were eerily silent as he patrolled. Every shadow seemed to hold a secret, every whisper a potential clue. Edward's senses were on high alert, knowing that the Ripper could be lurking around any corner.

As he moved through the dimly lit alleys around Mansell Street, he spotted the same red ink symbol on the door to the railway depot, The Watcher cautiously but with purpose moved into the dark winding corridors of the back offices. It was eerily quiet. He moved silently checking every corner, investigating every room.

"so you came?" a voice rang out echoing around the empty corridors in the darkness.

"SHOW YOURSELF!" Edward demanded, his order echoing back at him.

"as you wish Eddie" the voice replied.

Suddenly Edward heard a noise behind him, footsteps. Edward spun around as a figure emerged from the darkness. A man standing no more than two yards away, he stood motionless draped in an elegant black cloak and black top hat, his face covered by a dark scarf only revealing his maddened eyes. The dim light glinted off a knife in his hand. The Ripper, a spectre of death that had haunted the city, was finally within reach. Edward's heart raced as he prepared for the confrontation he had anticipated for so long.

"Your game ends now!" Edward growled with a rage that he felt burning in his very soul.

"No, it's far from over" The Ripper chuckled as he lunged forward slashing wildly with his blade.

The Watcher quickly and skilfully evaded the first slash of the knife but the second caught him on his upper left arm tearing his suit and ripping into his flesh. But he couldn't let the pain stop him. He immediately ducked under the Ripper's arm and delivered a strike with the silver handle of his cane to the bridge of the Ripper's nose. The Ripper let out a pained yelp but continued his frenzied attack.

The Watcher drew his sword from his cane and their blades collided. The clash was intense and chaotic. The Ripper was ruthless, but the Watcher was cunning, he matched The Ripper's every move. Blocking his slashes and stabs, and taking advantage of openings. Both managed to land blows and ruby droplets of blood speckled the floor. It was no longer just a battle of physical prowess but of wits and will. The Ripper fought with a bloodlust that the Watcher had never seen but in return, he fought with the determination of a man who knew that failure was not an option.

Amid their struggle, The Watcher managed to swipe his leg across, kicking the Ripper's feet out from under him and he fell to the floor with a mighty thud, The Ripper's knife clattered away into the darkness and the Watcher stood over him with the tip of his sword firmly pressed against the Ripper's throat.

"It's over" The Watcher panted breathlessly "I'm ending this now!" he bellowed, the rage still building behind his pale blue eyes.

"What? You going to kill me?" The Ripper sneered calmly "If you do, where's justice, Eddie?".

The Watcher felt his anger boiling over.

"You don't deserve to live after what you've done!" he shouted. "Those poor women you butchered, I would be doing this city a favour" he snarled, he could barely contain his vehement hatred for the man before him.

"you're right Eddie, I'm a murderer, a Monster, a blood-soaked demon from hell itself, so do it, I dare you, become a monster, I dare you, Eddie, I DARE YOU!" The Ripper began laughing maniacally. The Watcher couldn't contain his rage anymore, the faces of the victims flashed before him, and the gruesome scene from Miller's court seared into his memory. The Watcher raised his sword high above his head and letting out a primal scream brought it down with as much force as he could muster.

The Ripper fell silent.

The blade struck the ground by The Ripper's head.

"No," said the Watcher calmly "I'm taking you to Abberline, there will be Justice" he bent down grabbing the Ripper by the scuff of the neck.

The Ripper's eyes smiled above his dark face covering. "How predictable" He Sneered. Suddenly The Watcher felt searing pain. With a cunning manoeuvre, the Ripper had managed to get Edward to lower his guard and plunged a small, concealed dagger up under his armour plate and into his gut. The Watcher collapsed to his knees as the Ripper stood and dusted himself off, "This was fun Eddie, but I have never much liked the idea of living in the Tower, and I'm not fond of the idea of the hangman's noose either".

"You bastard!" The Watcher spluttered.

"Now, let's keep things civil" The Ripper ordered calmly behind smiling eyes. "This has been the most fun I've had in years, but I think I've had my fill of London. Plenty more cities out there and plenty more whores who need ripping".

"I won't let you get away with this!" Edward said through gritted teeth.

"How do you intend to stop me?" questioned the Ripper. "I'll tell you what." he continued "I'm not going to reveal your little secret, not yet at least, I'm not even going to kill you. I'm going to let you see the havoc I reap upon this world." The ripper began to laugh "Every time you hear of a murdered whore, you are going to think to yourself, was that Jack? Every woman I kill now, oh and there will be many, will be because you failed to stop me"

"This isn't over" Edward interrupted as he tried to get to his feet but collapsed down once again.

"Oh, but Eddie, I know, it's never going to be over, but you will never find me, not now, where's the fun in that?" And with those final words, the Ripper slipped away, disappearing into the labyrinth of Whitechapel's alleys. The Watcher pulling himself up bleeding heavily tried to chase after him, but it was in vain. The Ripper was gone, melting into the night like a ghost.

Breathing heavily and wounded, The Watcher realized the gravity of what had just happened. The Ripper had evaded capture again, slipping through his fingers like smoke. The streets of London were still not safe.

As he dragged himself back to Langley Manor, Edward felt a mix of frustration and determination. He had come so close to ending the reign of terror, only to be thwarted at the last moment. This battle with the Ripper had been lost, but the war was far from over.

In the solitude of his sanctuary, Edward patched himself up and pondered his next move. The Ripper's escape had complicated matters, but it had also strengthened Edward's resolve. He knew that The Watcher's mission was more important than ever. The people of London needed a guardian, someone to stand against the darkness that lurked in their city.

As the first light of dawn broke over the horizon, Edward Langley, knew that his journey was far from over. There would be more challenges ahead and more dangers to face. But he was ready. For the sake of London, for the memory of those lost to the Ripper's blade, he would continue to watch over the city, a silent sentinel in the night.

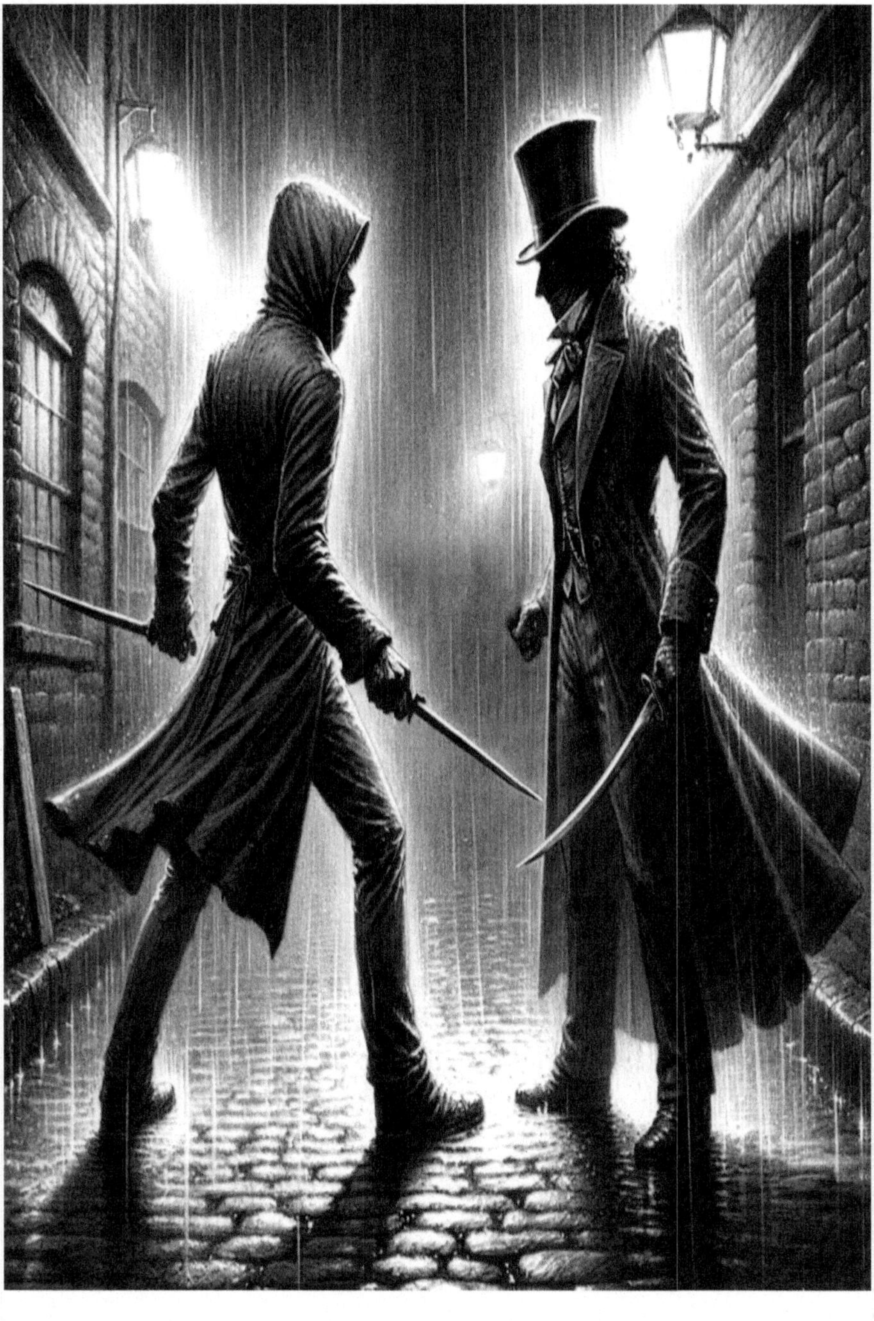

Chapter 15:
Dawn of the Watcher

As the first rays of dawn broke over the horizon, casting a soft light on the streets of London, Edward awoke in his sanctuary. His encounter with the Ripper had left him wounded with a deep sense of frustration, but also a renewed determination. The elusive killer had slipped through his grasp, but the night's events had solidified Edward's resolve to protect the city.

In the quiet of his sanctuary, Edward pondered the implications of the Ripper's escape. It was a stark reminder of the challenges he faced and the complexity of his mission. The city was still in danger, and the Ripper's game was far from over. Edward knew that he needed to be more vigilant, more resourceful, and more determined than ever.

The public's reaction to the sightings of The Watcher had become a mixture of fear, speculation, and intrigue. Edward realized that his actions as The Watcher were not only shaping the narrative of his nocturnal identity but also influencing the public's perception of justice and vigilantism.

As he spent the following days recovering and strategizing his next moves, Edward also had to navigate his life as a nobleman. The dual aspects of his existence were becoming increasingly difficult to balance. Yet, he understood that his position in society provided him with resources and access that were crucial to his mission.

Edward had managed to convince those close to him that his injury was from a robbery that had happened on a late-night walk. This fabricated tale seemed to have worked on everyone except the dutiful Mr. Humphrey who had listened to his master's story with a look of suspicion painted brazenly on his face.

It wasn't long before Edward had recovered enough to continue his social life. One evening, at a gathering of London's elite, Edward overheard conversations about The Watcher. Some there spoke of him as a hero, a beacon of hope in a city plagued by fear, while others debated the morality of his actions and the dangers of vigilantism. Edward listened, his expression neutral, but internally he grappled with the same questions.

Despite the doubts and the moral complexities, Edward's encounters with the citizens he had saved reaffirmed his purpose. Their gratitude, and their stories of survival, fuelled his commitment to continue his fight against the darkness that threatened London.

The Watcher's presence in the city had begun to change the dynamics of the underworld. Criminals were more cautious, and some were even deterred from committing their heinous acts. Edward's influence was becoming evident, and he knew that his role was making a difference.

However, the Ripper's continued freedom was a constant reminder of the battles yet to be fought. Edward realized that his journey as The Watcher was evolving into something greater than he had initially envisioned. It was no longer just about avenging the wronged or bringing individual criminals to justice; it was about safeguarding the city itself.

As the chapter of his life as The Watcher continued to unfold, Edward embraced his role with a newfound sense of purpose. He was not just a nobleman or a vigilante; he was a guardian of London, like his father before him, a symbol of hope and justice in a time of uncertainty and fear.

The dawn of The Watcher had arrived, and with it, a new era for the city of London. Amidst the challenges and dangers that lay ahead, Edward stood resolute, ready to face whatever the future held.

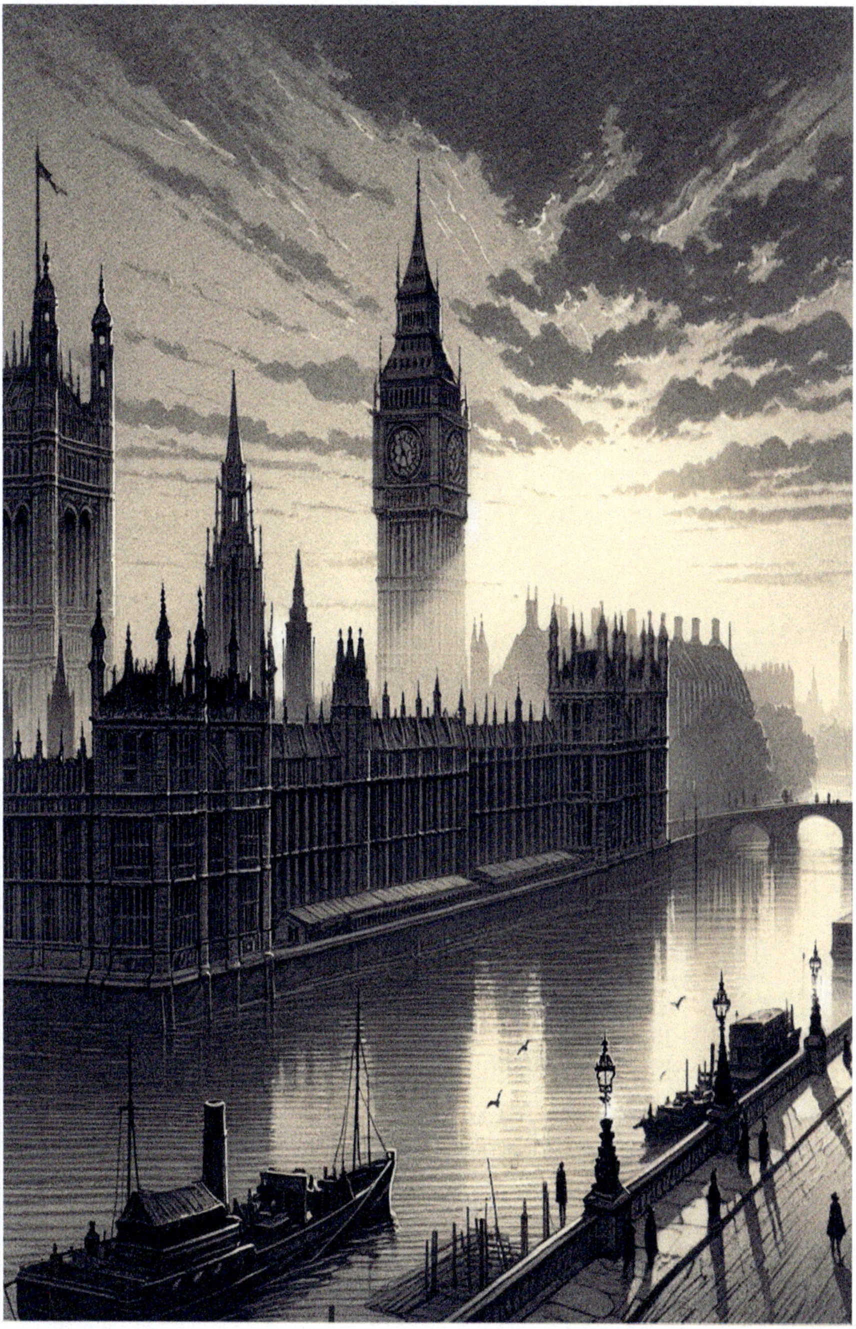

Epilogue:

Echoes of Tomorrow

Weeks passed since the night the Ripper had eluded capture, and the city of London continued to pulse with the rhythm of life, its heartbeat a blend of hope and apprehension. The Watcher, a shadowy figure who had become both a guardian and a mystery, remained a topic of hushed conversations in every corner of the city.

In Langley Manor, Edward stood before a large window overlooking the gardens, his thoughts introspective. The events of the past weeks had transformed him, not just as The Watcher, but as a man. He had faced darkness, both within the city and within himself, and had emerged with a deeper understanding of his purpose.

The Watcher had become more than a response to a moment of injustice; he was now a symbol of resilience, a testament to the power of one individual's resolve to make a difference. Edward's dual life, while challenging, had brought a sense of fulfilment he had never known. He had saved lives, brought hope to the hopeless, and inspired change in a city that had been on the brink of despair.

However, the echoes of the unresolved Ripper case lingered in his mind. Edward knew that the battle was far from over. There were still shadows that needed to be brought into the light, evils that lurked in the hidden corners of London.

As he turned away from the window, Edward's gaze fell upon his Watcher attire, neatly arranged in the secret chamber of his manor. It was a reminder of the commitment he had made, a commitment that extended beyond himself and into the future of the city he loved.

Edward knew that his journey would continue to be fraught with challenges and dangers. But as he prepared for another night's patrol, he felt a sense of clarity and determination. The Watcher was needed, now more than ever, and Edward Langley was ready to uphold that mantle.

As he stepped into the night, The Watcher blended into the darkness, a silent protector in a city of echoes and whispers. His presence was a promise, a vow that no matter what, there would always be a light guiding the way just as there will always be new threats trying to pull London into the shadows.

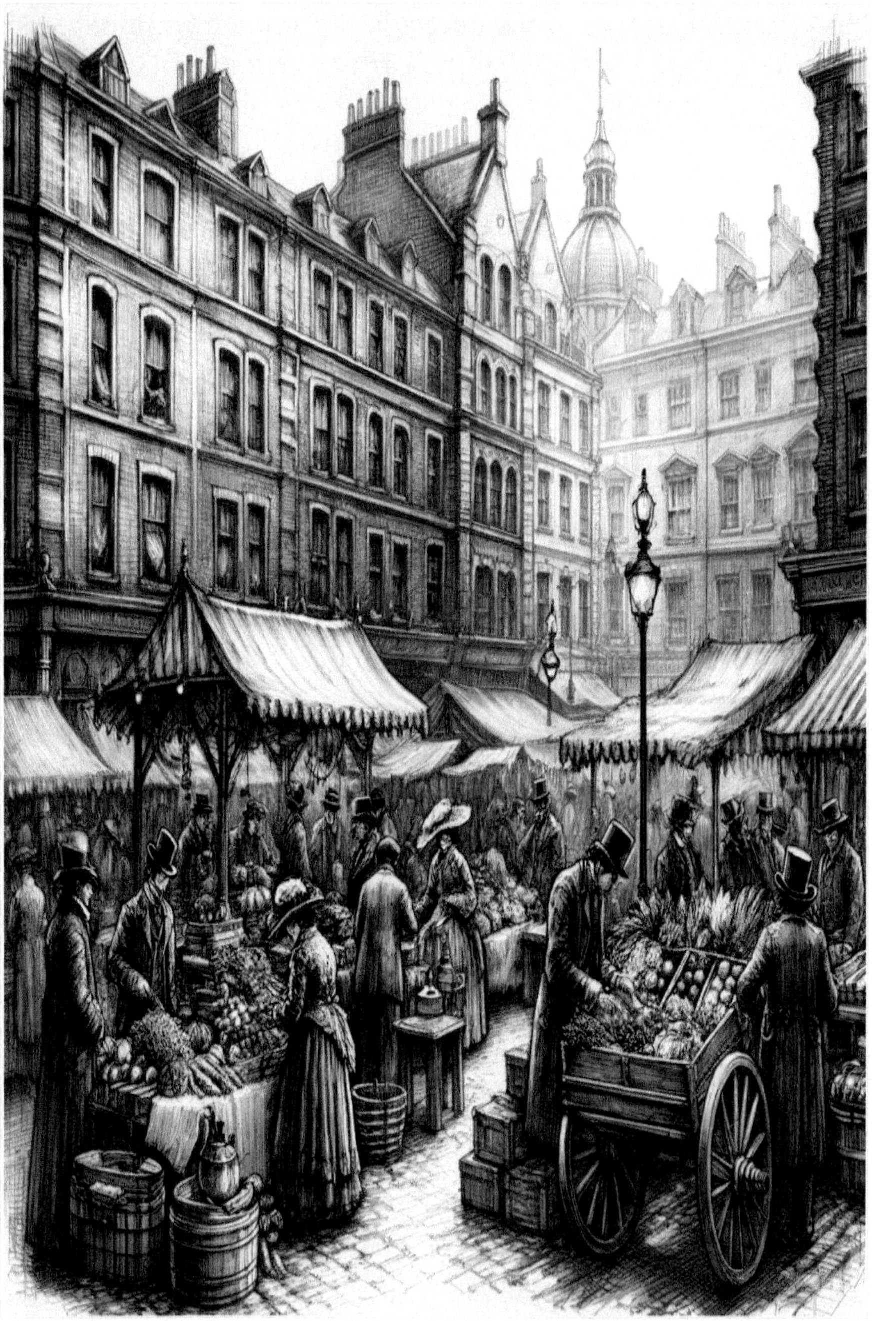

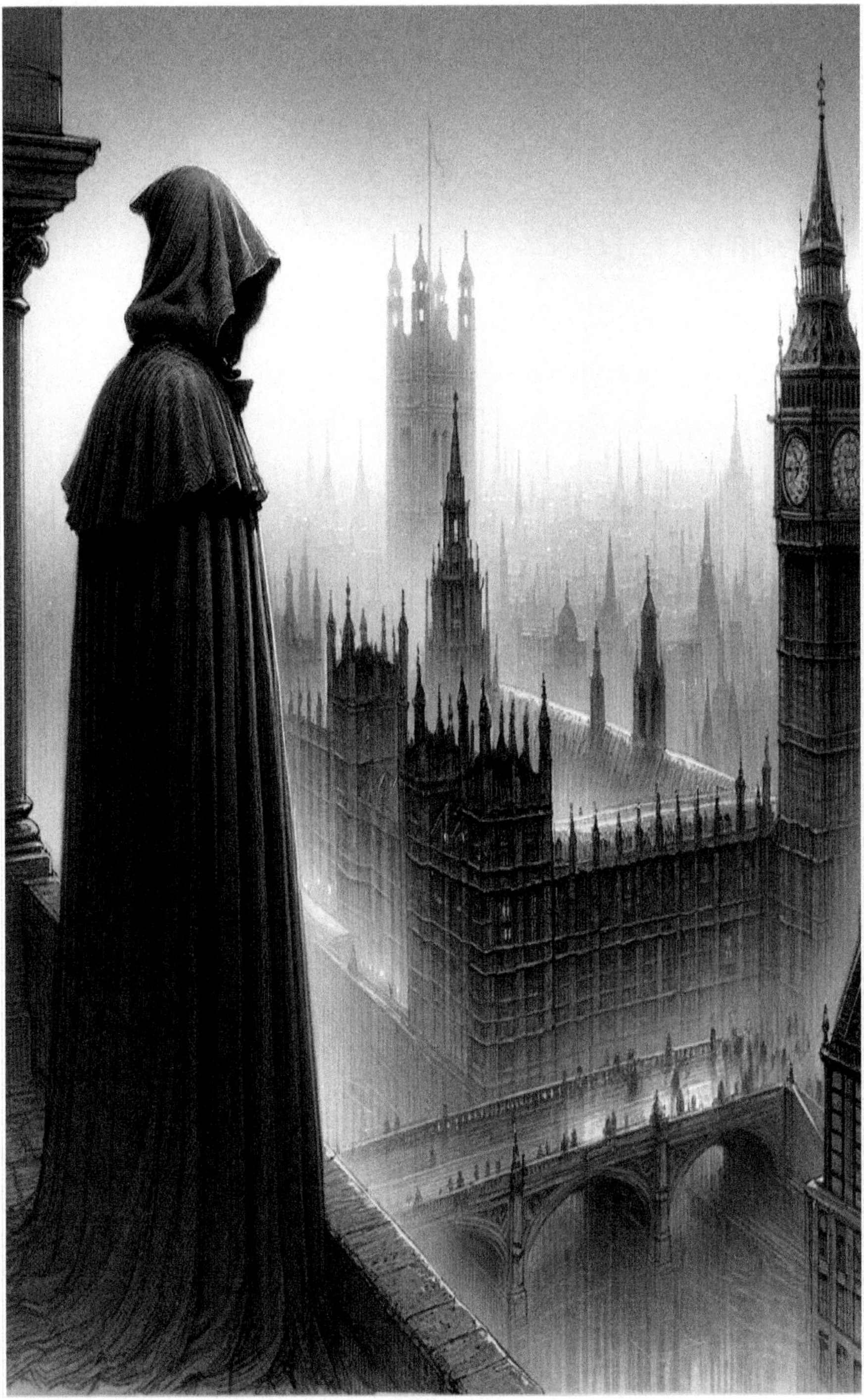

Printed in Great Britain
by Amazon